Night Sky

Susan Yankowitz

A SAMUEL FRENCH ACTING EDITION

FOUNDED 1830

SAMUELFRENCH.COM
SAMUELFRENCH-LONDON.CO.UK

FOR PRODUCTION ENQUIRIES

UNITED STATES AND CANADA
Info@SamuelFrench.com
1-866-598-8449

UNITED KINGDOM AND EUROPE
Theatre@SamuelFrench-London.co.uk
020-7255-4302

Each title is subject to availability from Samuel French, depending upon country of performance. Please be aware that *Night Sky* may not be licensed by Samuel French in your territory. Professional and amateur producers should contact the nearest Samuel French office or licensing partner to verify availability.

MUSIC USE NOTE

IMPORTANT BILLING AND CREDIT REQUIREMENTS

NIGHT SKY was produced by the Women's Project & Productions under the directorship of Julia Miles at the Judith Anderson Theatre, New York City, from May 14-June 9, 1991. It was directed by Joseph Chaikin with the following cast:

DANIEL . . . . Edward Baran

BILL . . . . Tom Cayler

ANNA . . . . Joan MacIntosh

SPEECH THERAPIST AND OTHERS . . . . Aleta Mitchell

APHASIC PATIENT AND OTHERS . . . . Paul Zimet

JENNIFER . . . . Lizabeth Zindel

Set Design by George Xenos
Lighting Design by Beverly Emmons
Costume Design by Mary Brecht
Sound Design by Mark Bennett
Stage Management by Ruth Kreshka
Casting by Susan Haskins

In the spring of 2009, a revised version of the play was produced Off-Broadway by Stan Raiff / Power Productions in association with The National Aphasia Association. It was directed by Daniella Topol with the following cast:

ANNA . . . . Jordan Baker

JENNIFER . . . . Lauren Ashley Carter

APHASIC PATIENT AND OTHERS . . . . Dan Domingues

BILL . . . . Tuck Milligan

SPEECH THERAPIST AND OTHERS . . . . Maria-Christina Oliveras

DANIEL . . . . Jim Stanek

Set Design by Cameron Anderson
Costume Design by Katherine Roth
Lighting by Peter West
Sound Design by Daniel Baker and Aaron Meicht/
Broken Chord Collective
Stage Management by Carlos Maisonet
Casting by Geoff Josselson

CHARACTERS

ANNA – an astronomer, in her 40s; strong, intelligent and intense; moves from extreme self-confidence to extreme vulnerability in course of play. The role requires vocal and physical stylization plus the ability to convey a wide range of emotions.

DANIEL – **ANNA**'s live-in lover, younger than she by 5 years; opera singer, baritone (*see note below); warm, outgoing, playful, loving, and sensual.

JENNIFER – **ANNA**'s daughter, 16; bright, sarcastic, self-dramatizing and tender-hearted – a very contemporary teen-ager.

BILL – **ANNA**'s astronomer colleague, 45-60; socially clumsy but imaginative and charismatic in the classroom.

SPEECH THERAPIST – and other female roles; 30's-50's: Articulate, patient, empathic and skilled in active listening. Versatility and a flair for creating a variety of convincing characters are essential to the role.

APHASIC PATIENT – and other male roles (including young man at dance); 25-35. The role requires improvisatory skills, vocal calisthenics and ease with non-naturalistic performance styles.

* Because **DANIEL** is an opera singer, it is ideal to cast an actor with a fine voice so that his career seems credible. However, it is even more important to have an excellent actor in the role so if a choice is necessary, please consider the acting requirements over the vocal ones: tapes can, if necessary, be used as support, enhancement or substitutes. And except for the "*Papageno*" aria in Scene 9, all other music sung by **DANIEL** can be selected by the actor and director.

THE SET

Encompassing both naturalistic and abstract elements, the set for *NIGHT SKY* needs to be imaginatively reconceived for each theatrical space. The play takes place – sometimes simultaneously – in various rooms of a middle-class apartment, on the street, in a classroom, a hospital, a school gymnasium, and conference hall. These should be suggested and defined by lights and well-chosen objects rather than by any attempt at verisimilitude. Fluidity of movement from scene to scene is far more important than furniture. Platforms and levels can be used to enhance flexibility, and very specific lighting is essential.

Video can be used creatively, too, especially to render the 'magical mystery tour' of the night sky.

THE COSTUMES

Because several actors play many roles, and because most characters move quickly from one scene to another, costumes also need to be adaptable. Each performer should have a basic outfit to which accessories – somewhat stylized, in keeping with the tone of the play – can be added as needed. All design elements in the play should feel contemporary.

NOTE ON PERIOD AND PLACE

This play should always take place in the present, which means that any dates or slang will need to be updated for production. When performed outside of America, it is better to adapt the references and idioms to the language of that country. The themes of the play are universal and will have more immediacy when linguistically connected to the time, place, performers and audience.

PERFORMANCE TIME

NIGHT SKY runs a bit more than 1 and ½ hours, plus one intermission.

INTRODUCTION

As a writer, I am very often drawn to the drama of people in extreme situations, people pushed by fate or accident or character to the edge of some abyss, personal or political. When Joseph Chaikin asked me to write a play about his own extreme condition – aphasia, or speechlessness – it coincided with a nightmare of my own and one which I know I share with many others: the terror of being locked in the self, unable to communicate. Joe anticipated that this theme would seduce me – and it did.

After the stroke that devastated his ability to speak, Joe could utter only a few disjointed words. He was unable to read or write. His memory for names, places, and numbers was impaired; abstract thought, which had always been his primary form of intellectual and creative inquiry, eluded him. During a long and arduous recovery, he began to assemble a vocabulary and finally, a new means of expression without conventional syntax, often lacking connective words like conjunctions and prepositions but nonetheless comprehensible, even poetic and profound, an idiosyncratic language which *could* communicate – but only if one listened in a manner equally new. What I came to understand was that the mind of the aphasic remains intact but the route from brain to mouth, no longer direct, is like a minefield.

Because Joe asked that the central character be an astronomer, I began doing research on both aphasia and astronomy, and discovered the extraordinary metaphor upon which the play is built, the almost perfect symmetry between the black holes in the universe and the dark matter of the brain, both of them filled with light (comprehension and thought) which is trapped inside, paradoxically invisible and present at the same time.

Embracing both the stars and the domestic, *NIGHT SKY* is about language, about inner and outer space, about a medical condition, a family's ordeal, and the resiliency of the human spirit as it meets unexpected challenges: in Anna's new language, like

> "…Alice Wonderland,
> fall down black hole,
> not dying but ex-plore new world."

It was inspired by Joe, and written for him, with infinite love and respect.

– *Susan Yankowitz, 2010*

ACKNOWLEDGEMENTS

The playwright wishes to express her gratitude for the invaluable support and collaboration of the many organizations and individuals who helped in the development of this piece. A grant from TCG provided the means for a stimulating workshop in A.C.T.'s Plays-in-Process series. A Playwrights' Center McKnight fellowship enabled a fruitful collaboration with The Illusion Theatre in Minneapolis, under the sensitive direction of Martha Boesing. New Dramatists supplied much-needed space for early explorations and a reading. Dr. Martha Sarno at The Rusk Institute assisted with medical information. William Alschuler was a bountiful resource in the area of astronomy. Julia Miles and The Women's Project were the first to produce the work in New York; fifteen years later, Ellayne Ganzfried of NAA brought the script to Stan Raiff, which resulted in a new Off-Broadway production.

Of the others, too numerous to mention, whose talents and insights contributed to the work's creation, I would like especially to thank Joyce Aaron, Noreen Barnes, Len Berkman, Lillian Butler, Shami Chaikin, Bill Coco, Ed Gueble and San Francisco State University, Tori Haring-Smith, Irene Kling, and above all Herbert Leibowitz, who has seen almost every production and lent his editorial wisdom and life-saving love to every revision.

"Perhaps someone with expert knowledge of the human brain will understand my illness, discover what a brain injury does to a man's mind, memory and body...I know there is a great deal of talk now about the cosmos and outer space, and that our earth is just a minute particle of this infinite universe. But actually, people rarely think about this; the most they can imagine are flights to the nearest planets revolving around the sun. As for the flight of a bullet, or a shell or bomb fragment, that rips open a man's skull, splitting and burning the tissues of his brain, crippling his memory, sight, hearing, awareness – these days people don't find anything extraordinary in that..."

– L. Zazestsy, wounded in the head during
the battle of Smolensk, 1943

Scene One

(Everywhere, encompassing and unifying the audience and performance area, is the vivid, star-filled night sky.)

*(**ANNA** too stands within it, on a podium, completing a lecture to her class.)*

ANNA. ...but what we see represents only ten percent – possibly only one percent – of what exists. Most of the universe is hidden, invisible to us still, a mysterious absence. We know very little. Even the most basic insights elude us. How many stars are there, and how do we know there aren't more? Why do the planets rotate and is it possible they could stop? If black holes are truly black and truly holes, how can we be sure they're there? And within all that dark matter, somewhere, does life exist?

(pause)

These are the questions we'll be considering in the next few weeks. The word "consider," by the way – did you know that it comes from Latin and means literally "with the stars?" All languages are filled with these references. When you miss your class because you have the flu – "influenza" – that derives from the Italian for "astral influence." And if your friend calls you a "schlimazel" for spilling wine on your white suit? That's Yiddish for someone born under an unlucky star. Then there's "disaster!" a word we hear all too often these days, attached to hurricanes, floods, and even our economy – and what does "dis-aster" actually mean? Bad star!

(steps down from the podium)

Class dismissed!

(The stars go out; the stage goes black.)

(Lights up in ANNA*'s living room.)*

*(*DANIEL, ANNA*'s partner, is playing solitaire on his
PDA.* JENNIFER, *her daughter, is drawing in a sketch
pad.)*

ANNA. *(entering)* Home from the wars.

JENNIFER. Yeah, we know. The star wars. Hi, Mom.

ANNA. *(putting away her coat, briefcase, etc.)* Hi, sweetheart.
Sweethearts. Sorry I'm late.

JENNIFER. No problema.

ANNA. Mucho problema. Problemas. I didn't pick up the
cleaning. I didn't go to the bakery. I didn't buy printer
paper – or toilet paper.

DANIEL. No toilet paper?! Oh shit!

ANNA. *(starting to set up her laptop)* I'd need six hands and
ten brains to handle everything that came at me today.
And finally, finally, I'm all packed up and ready to
leave my office when I hear a knock at the door. It's a
student in my lecture class – tears cascading down her
cheeks. The calamity? She thought she'd registered
for astrology!

JENNIFER. So she's dropping?

ANNA. *(opening her laptop)* Oh no. We bonded. Turns out
we're both Aquarians. Of course I don't really know
what that means but it can't be good. I had an email
from the Astronomy Journal saying I have to get my
revisions in by tomorrow morning. I thought I had
another week, but…I don't. So – sorry – there's nothing in the fridge and I'll have to work all night, which
means that you two –

JENNIFER. Hey, Mom, chill. We ordered pizza.

ANNA. Great! I'm starving.

JENNIFER. Well…I mean…like, we didn't know when you
were coming home and we sort of…scarfed it down.

ANNA. You didn't.

DANIEL. Sorry, hon.

ANNA. Listen. I'm going to be late twice a week this semester. It would really help if you guys cooked dinner on those nights.

JENNIFER. I can't. No way, mom. Not with calculus and French and volleyball and model U.N. plus maybe a social life. Daniel, you do it.

DANIEL. Me? Uh-uh. No talent in the kitchen. You know that.

(pause)

Not much talent anywhere, I guess.

ANNA. Ohhhh. City Opera! What happened?

DANIEL. I sang my audition piece, they asked if I had something else, so I gave them the Puccini…

ANNA. They wanted to hear more. That sounds good. Very good.

DANIEL. I thought so, too. But when I finished, one of them said that my voice was a little thin in the low notes.

ANNA. Thin? No! Do you think it was?

DANIEL. …I don't know. Maybe…

(concentrates again on his PDA and keeps playing whenever he can withdraw)

JENNIFER. Mom, tomorrow…after volleyball…I'm going with Francesca to get a tattoo.

ANNA. No. No, you're not getting a tattoo.

JENNIFER. Just a tiny one, right over my ankle bone, sort of like an ankle bracelet, but with really sick colors, you know.

ANNA. Sick is right. The dyes can get into your bloodstream. No.

JENNIFER. Omigod, Mom, that's so middle ages! Nobody gets infected these days! We know the good places to go. And my design is like unbelievable! You'll love it. Look.

(shows what she's been drawing: a band of stars)

JENNIFER. *(cont.)* See? Orion's belt. But around my ankle. Sort of in honor of you. How cool is that??

ANNA. Way cool, crazy cool, whatever you kids say – but if you want to honor me, try getting on honor roll this year. ...Don't you have homework?

JENNIFER. Tons.

ANNA. Then hop to it.

(JENNIFER *mockingly hops off. To* **DANIEL***:*)

I don't get it. You've sung those arias all over the country. To rave reviews.

DANIEL. Yeah. They're wild for me in St. Louis, Sarasota, DC – but this is New York, babe. You know what the competition is like here. So. ...I was nervous. Very nervous.

ANNA. Well, that'll do it.

DANIEL. Do what?

ANNA. Mess you up. When you go into an audition or give a lecture, you have to be on top of everything, radiate confidence.

DANIEL. Like you.

ANNA. Hey. I'm not trying to put you down.

DANIEL. You don't have to. I'm already down. You're kicking me.

ANNA. You want to stay down? You can't. You're giving that recital in a few weeks. And scouts come to these things, don't they? From Germany, Italy – maybe even the Met...?

DANIEL. Yeah, sometimes. So?

ANNA. So – go for it! Rehearse, work the low notes if they're weak –

DANIEL. I will, I will. *(concentrates more intently on the PDA)* First. Thing. Tomorrow.

ANNA. Tomorrow? What's wrong with tonight?

DANIEL. I'm on a roll now, babe. Can't you see? I'm winning.

ANNA. *(looking at game)* At solitaire?!

(grabs it out of his hands)

How can you waste yourself on that crap?

DANIEL. Leave me to my small triumphs, please!

(They tussle over the PDA and end up in each other's arms: sex becomes subtext, then text.)

*(In her room, **JENNIFER** practices French conjugations, continuing under the scene.)*

JENNIFER. *Je parlerai. Tu parleras. Il/elle/on parlera. Nous parlerons. Vous parlerez. Ils/elles parleront. Je mangerai. Tu mangeras. Il/elle/on mangera. Nous mangerons. Vous mangerez. Ils/elles mangeront. Je comprenerai. ETC.*

ANNA. I just want to help…

DANIEL. Well, I have a few ideas on how you might do that.

(begins to caress her)

ANNA. This is your solution to everything.

DANIEL. It seems to work for you, too.

ANNA. *(a little seduced, a little seductive)* I have my little weaknesses, what can I say?

DANIEL. Don't say anything. Let your body do the talking.

(Touches her more intimately. She responds, then hesitates.)

ANNA. We can't… Jenny…

DANIEL. Jenny's studying French. What could be more conducive?

ANNA. …I have so much to do, though. Hours and hours of revisions. And you, you really should be rehearsing…

DANIEL. But oo-la-la, I'm so much better at…French.

(They kiss; she finally pulls away.)

ANNA. I can't, I wish I could, but I can't. …Rain date?

DANIEL. Good idea. Fantastic idea! We're supposed to have a downpour tonight.

ANNA. Tonight???

DANIEL. Around midnight. There will be no escape from Don Giovanni then!

ANNA. Did I ever tell you that you have the most adorable smile?

DANIEL. *(vampirish)* And did I ever tell *you* that you have the most delectable...throat?

(hands her a gift box)

I bought it after the audition. Instead of shooting myself.

ANNA. I'm speechless.

DANIEL. Well, that's a new one!

ANNA. *(takes out a string of large colorful beads)* Oh, Daniel – they're fabulous. I'll wear them to your concert.

(He helps her put them on.)

DANIEL. *(still the vampire)* You'll wear them tonight! The beads – and nothing else.

ANNA. What a rich fantasy life you have.

DANIEL. You don't know the half of it. So – we have a date?

ANNA. Yes, yes. *If* I get this work finished.

DANIEL. You will. And when the chimes peal at midnight and the rain pours down, I will pour myself into...*you.*

(a last embrace; as he leaves the room)

What are you going to do about dinner?

ANNA. Ohhh... Toss me an apple.

(He does, then goes to his studio, begins to vocalize and rehearse his aria. ANNA bites into the apple and starts working on her laptop. JENNIFER continues her conjugations. It's noisy and chaotic. A knock on the door:)

Who's there?

BILL. Bill.

(She opens the door.)

You weren't expecting me? It's Thursday, isn't it? Thursday at eight?

ANNA. Oh no. I mean yes, I guess it is. Sorry.

BILL. I perceive a cloud of dark, dark, very dark matter around your head. How bad were they?

ANNA. The worst yet. I gave a quiz on Tuesday, just to find out what they knew. Two of them thought that *Galileo* was hit on the head by an apple and '*invented*' gravity. I asked which was more important to human life, the sun or the moon. One guy said it was obviously the moon, because the moon shines at night when we can't see without its help, while the poor superfluous sun casts light during the day when who the hell needs it??!

BILL. And I'm teaching the next two classes…!

ANNA. You'll have to pull out all your tricks.

BILL. I've got one all ready. A riddle. "How does the solar system hold up its pants?"

JENNIFER. *(already half-way into the room)* With Orion's belt!

*(**BILL** is mightily chagrined.)*

Hi, Bill. *Maman! Au secours! Francais. Examen. Demain. Demain est la futur. Examen dans la tense futur. Je suis perdu.*

ANNA. Pardon?

JENNIFER. The future, Mom, hello?! Like, I don't know it.

ANNA. Well, who does?

BILL. What's up, Jen?

JENNIFER. Placement test tomorrow. In French. It's huge! If I don't pass, I don't get into AP and if I don't get into AP my record looks like sh – crapola, and I'll end up in some boondock college and naturally I'll start drinking and taking drugs because I'll have zero self-esteem and then–

BILL. Hey. Don't look at me. I studied Russian.

JENNIFER. Mom! You gotta help me. This could be an epic fail. Like, I'm totally stressed out.

ANNA. Stress is a part of life. Just drill yourself. Grammar is not brain surgery.

BILL. Anna, can we go over your lesson plan for next month?

ANNA. Not now, I can't, I'm really sorry – I *have* to meet this deadline, but I do have a hard copy you can see…. And we'll talk on the weekend, okay?

(rummages through her briefcase till she finds it; gives it to him; while:)

JENNIFER. I will be. *Je serai.* You will be. *Tu seras.* He will be, she will be, one will be: I*l/elle/on…sera*? Is that it? *Sera*? No, that's Italian. Or maybe Spanish? "*Che sera, sera,* whatever will be will be." Do you know that song, Ma?

(ANNA nods.)

So do you think it *is sera*? The same in Spanish and Italian and French? Could be, couldn't it?

ANNA. Maybe. …'*Elle sera malade.*' She will be sick. Yes, '*sera*.' I think that's right.

JENNIFER. But you're not a hundred per cent?

ANNA. I haven't studied French in ages. See if Daniel can help you.

JENNIFER. He doesn't know French.

ANNA. Yes, he does. He sings whole operas in French.

JENNIFER. The words, yeah, but he doesn't know what they mean.

ANNA. That's ridiculous. He couldn't sing anything if he didn't understand the meaning.

JENNIFER. He's got a translation that gives him the gist but word for word, trust me, he doesn't have a clue.

BILL. *(looking at the lesson plan)* Anna… Redshifts? The electromagnetic spectrum? You think these kids are up to it?

ANNA. They have to be.

(to JENNIFER)

Why don't you just use your textbook?

JENNIFER. I left it in my locker.

(noting ANNA*'s incredulous expression)*

Yeah, I know, like I'm brain-dead.

ANNA. Then go on line and get what you need.

(calls out)

...Daniel, can you tone it down a little, please?

JENNIFER. You don't care if I fail, do you?

ANNA. Haven't you heard of the Copernican Revolution, young lady? For your information, the earth does not revolve around you.

JENNIFER. Right, mom. It revolves around *you!*

(storms out, upset)

ANNA. Honestly, Bill, I'm over my head.

JENNIFER. *(yelling over her shoulder) Out* of your head!

BILL. *(shouting back) Over* your head! Over *most* heads – including mine.

(JENNIFER*'s door slams.)*

ANNA. Do I hear self-deprecation? From you?

BILL. *I* wasn't invited to give a paper at the conference. *I'm* not representing the United States of America. Everyone at school reeks of envy.

ANNA. Not you, though.

BILL. Me? No. Well, maybe a little. Well, maybe a lot.

ANNA. You? The star of the department? The only teacher who's always over-enrolled?

BILL. That's true...

(picks up two apples)

So let's see. I'm popular in the classroom. You'll be world famous.

(juggles the apples)

The classroom, the world... Classroom, world... Oh, all right. I'll trade places with you. Just say the word.

ANNA. *(laughing)* The word is 'goodbye.' If I don't get back to these damn revisions, I'll be in deep deep bleep bleep. I'll see you in the observatory on Saturday. Oh, and don't forget about Daniel's concert. We have to fill the hall. Check out the email reminder I sent and forward it to your own list, will you?

BILL. Sure. He sounds great.

ANNA. He is. But too loud. …See you.

> (**BILL** *exits,* **ANNA** *settles back to work.* **DANIEL** *sings more powerfully. She tries but can't blot out the sound. Calls out again:)*

> Daniel! It's terrific! Just turn down the volume!

> *(no response; tries to work but can't as his voice becomes even stronger)*

> Please!!! I can't concentrate!

> *(He keeps singing. Finally she goes to his door and yells:)*

> Daniel, I can't hear myself think!!!

DANIEL. *(entering)* Were you calling me?

ANNA. Your voice – it drowns out everything!

DANIEL. What do you expect me to do? Mouth the words?

ANNA. You have no idea how distracting it is.

DANIEL. First you complain that I don't rehearse. Then you complain that I do.

ANNA. I'll never get this work done with all that noise!

DANIEL. *(stung)* Noise?! Are you referring to my music? my voice?

ANNA. You said you'd sound-proof that room.

DANIEL. I will. But get off my back. It's not my fault you missed your deadline.

ANNA. You know the first weeks of class are always a nightmare! You could have helped me out. I gave you the manuscript weeks ago. All you needed to do was circle the typos and make notes if something didn't make sense.

DANIEL. I tried. I did. But *nothing* made sense. How many times do I have to explain that those scientific words are Greek to me? And who are you to complain? You still can't tell the difference between a *roulade* and a *tessitura*. You don't even listen when I sing.

ANNA. I do listen. I just don't have a good ear. You know that.

DANIEL. I've told you again and again that you can train your ear.

ANNA. And you can train your mind! There's no reason why you can't understand my ideas. All kinds of people – even children! – are interested in the latest discoveries about the universe.

DANIEL. Oh. I see. In your corner, The Great Magnificent Mysterious Cosmos – and in mine, The Little Singer That Could. Maybe.

ANNA. That's not what I meant…!

DANIEL. Give it up, Anna. You think my work is shit.

ANNA. No. Just your vocabulary.

DANIEL. You turn everything around.

ANNA. Not your career.

DANIEL. You know, Anna, you're a bitch.

ANNA. You know, Daniel, you're a loser.

(dead silence except for:)

JENNIFER. *(under scene; in her room) J'aimerais.* I will love. *Tu aimeras. Il/elle/on* a*imera.*

ANNA. I'm sorry.

(no response from him)

I'm sorry! Please. I don't want to fight. You just don't realize how much I have on my mind.

DANIEL. Your mind, your mind – that's all you think about!

JENNIFER. *(as before) Nous aimerons. Vous aimerez. Ils/elles/ons aimeront.*

ANNA. Is that so? The greatest philosophers have argued endlessly about whether it's possible for a mind to think about itself, and–

(snaps her fingers)

– eureka! *You* solve the conundrum of centuries.

DANIEL. This is your favorite activity, isn't it? Brainstorming with yourself.

ANNA. What choice do I have? There's no other brain here to storm with.

JENNIFER. *(continuing through end of scene with conjugations in future tense) Je parlerai.* I will speak. ETC.

Je mangerai. I will eat. ETC.

Je dormirai. I will sleep. ETC.

Je finirai. I will finish. ETC.

DANIEL. I am more than a brain! Here. Feel that?

(grabs her hand against his chest)

It's a heart – and a heartbeat, in case you're interested.

ANNA. In case *you're* interested, hearts are controlled by the brain!

DANIEL. Do you always need to have the last word?!

ANNA. I don't have the first word! I haven't written a thing since I walked in the door! Scientists say that chaos is a higher form of order, but they haven't visited our house!

DANIEL. *(exploding)* And they won't! Keep them out of my life. I am going back into my studio to rehearse – and you, hot shot, you can take your chaos and your stars and your brainstorms and go to hell!

(slams out of the room)

ANNA. All right, I'm going!

(grabs her briefcase/laptop and dashes from the house. Lights go out. In the darkness.)

JENNIFER. *J'rai.* I will go. ETC.

Je dirai. I will say. ETC.

Je serai. I will be. ETC.

*(She continues her conjugations; **DANIEL** practices his aria.)*

(Suddenly, two bright headlights pierce the darkness. There is the screech of brakes and the thud of a body; all

the sounds are amplified and jumbled together as **ANNA**
is hit by a car.)

*(In the light shed by the headlights, her beads, the string
broken on impact, roll and scatter everywhere, a visual
replica of what is happening to her speech.)*

(Over the rolling beads, the **DOCTOR'S VOICE** *is heard,
overpowering and obliterating both the aria and JEN-
NY'S conjugations.)*

DOCTOR'S VOICE. *(as if into a recording device; pauses
between phrases)* Severe injury to left hemisphere of
brain between primary auditory cortex and angular
gyrus.   Profound damage to the language center
and all language functions, expressive and receptive,
including anomia   alexia   agraphia   apraxia...

(Dimly visible in the background, the **APHASIC PATIENT**
sits in a wheelchair, picking up phrases of the **DOC-
TOR***'s report – a speech anomaly called echolalia. [N.B:
During this sequence, the actor may improvise, creating
a musical counterpoint to the words he echoes or man-
gles. The following are only suggestions. Throughout the
play, he functions as a kind of Greek chorus, embodying
various forms of aphasia.])*

APHASIC PATIENT. A pax – prax- praxia – – see ya! See ya!

DOCTOR'S VOICE. Impairment of speech, reading, writing,
and verbal comprehension –

APHASIC PATIENT. *(overlapping)* ...erbal tention re reten-
tion...

DOCTOR'S VOICE. – especially abstractions and words per-
taining to time and positions in space.   Fragmented
syntax –

APHASIC PATIENT. ...frag sin – sin tax – tax...

DOCTOR'S VOICE. – disturbances in word retrieval and
reduction of functional vocabulary.

APHASIC PATIENT. ...func vobabble babbulary...

DOCTOR'S VOICE. Memory loss, disorientation, and multiple deficits of perception common to aphasia.

APHASIC PATIENT. ...com apha-sia...apha-sia......

> (DANIEL *and* JENNIFER *enter, holding flowers.*)

DANIEL. Aphasia?

APHASIC PATIENT. *(cheerfully)* Aphaaaa-sia.

> *(He wheels himself away as, in the glare of headlights, a hospital bed is wheeled in.* **ANNA**, *head bandaged, is propped against the pillows.*)

JENNIFER. *(going to* **ANNA**) Hi, Mom.

> *(*ANNA *doesn't seem to recognize her.*)

> Mom. Look. Your faves. Asters. Asters for stars, right? We brought 'em for you.

> *(gives her the flowers)*

ANNA. *(as if speaking absolutely intelligibly)* Gee kidge syzzzz dibble dibbledibble bodeebo!

JENNIFER. Mom?!

DANIEL. Anna?

> *(*ANNA *smiles, looks at flowers, not sure what to do with them, then decides that they are food and puts them in her mouth, eats.*)

> *(*DANIEL *and* JENNIFER *stare, incredulous.*)

> *(At the same time: in the classroom, lights up on* **BILL**, *just as he finishes pumping up a helium globe of the cosmos. It bursts with a blast of sound. From inside, glittering stars shoot upward like fireworks and spew everywhere.*)

BILL. And *that's* how it happened! Thirteen or fourteen billion years ago, the universe suddenly exploded in the Big Bang, the greatest mystery we know, an incredible cosmic accident – and what had once been pure energy split into millions of bits and pieces spinning through space – an old order destroyed and everything beginning again, utterly strange and new...

Scene Two

(A series of vignettes, defined by lighting, each like an X-ray.)

THE THIRD DAY

(In the hosptial: **ANNA,** *in bed, is listening to herself as she tries out her voice, like someone singing a few notes aloud to hear how she sounds.)*

ANNA. Gridge sac dibble foojimigu – fooji – ?

(hearing that she's speaking gibberish; disbelieving)

Huh?

(tries again)

Ake dis looloo I me bunder –
Huh?? Huh??

(appalled; trying again, very slowly this time)

I ghimma babba inbane mebane...

(desperate)

Huh?! Huh??! Huhhhh?!!!

THE FOURTH DAY

*(***DANIEL*** enters for his first visit. Whatever he does,* **ANNA** *imitates. He smiles; she smiles in return. He takes her hand; she takes his. He pats her cheek; she pats his cheek, ETC.)*

DANIEL. How are you, sweetheart?
ANNA. ...Goo.
DANIEL. ...Goo?
ANNA. I...goo...glue.
DANIEL. You...glue?
ANNA. ...Glue...oooo.
DANIEL. *(pondering)* ...I glue...

(He starts to laugh; she starts to laugh.)

DANIEL. *(cont)* I…glue you, too.

(They laugh together. The laughter turns to tears. Only after they have been crying separately do they reach for each other.)

THE SIXTH DAY

(ANNA slowly dangles her legs off the bed, preparing to walk.)

(The APHASIC PATIENT is seated in a wheelchair near her room, practicing a sentence. [N.B.: His speech is always a bit more advanced than ANNA's.])

APHASIC PATIENT. Ame…isBoo

Brame…Booboo!

My ame brame is…Booboo. Boo-hoo. Boo – booce. *(etc.)*

(ANNA slides off the bed. She doesn't yet realize that her right side is quite weak. She takes a step or two and falls – right into the APHASIC PATIENT's lap. He is thrilled – and the word catapults right out of him.)

Boo-ruce! Bruce!

THE EIGHTH DAY

(The SPEECH THERAPIST is holding up a blackboard with "ANNA" written on it.)

SPEECH THERAPIST. This is your name. Can you tell me what it is?

(ANNA can't find it in her mind.)

Your name is…

(ANNA can't find it.)

Your name is Aaaaa…

ANNA. Aaaaaa…

SPEECH THERAPIST. *(pointing to the letters)* Aaa...nnaaa...

ANNA. Naaaa...

> *(The* **SPEECH THERAPIST** *continues trying to get* **ANNA** *to pronounce her name.* **ANNA** *can only manage one syllable at a time.)*

> *(At the same time:* **BILL** *is on the phone with* **DANIEL***.)*

BILL. She can't speak clearly? Can't always understand what's said to her? Can't read or write?

DANIEL. That's right.

BILL. Then what goes on inside her head?

DANIEL. She can't tell me, Bill.

BILL. But...can she think?

DANIEL. Can people think without words? I have no idea.

BILL. Well, you, you think in music, don't you? Maybe she's thinking in pictures, in star charts...

DANIEL. Maybe. But isn't that the kind of question you scientists study?

BILL. Will she be able to teach again?

DANIEL. I don't know. Why don't you visit and see for yourself?

BILL. *(avoiding the last comment)* Is she the same person? I mean, is she different on the outside but the same inside? Or different on the outside *and* the inside? Do you think she feels different to herself?

DANIEL. I told you, Bill! I don't know!!!

THE TENTH DAY

> *(At home:* **JENNIFER** *is rehearsing for her first private visit with her mother;* **DANIEL.** *plays* **ANNA***.)*

JENNIFER. So. ...Hi, Mom.

> *(***DANIEL** *smiles, waves.)*

> How ya doin'?

> *(***DANIEL** *'s expression becomes doleful.)*

> Not so hot, huh?

DANIEL. 'Glue…sidge…I bane – '

JENNIFER. She can talk better than that! She can say a few words. You told me she could.

DANIEL. Very few. …'Annn – naaa… Good!!'

JENNIFER. Good…? What's good?? Oh god, I can't do this! I don't know what to say!

DANIEL. Talk about yourself. What's going on. Try to act natural.

JENNIFER. Natural? Get real!

DANIEL. Can't get realer than this, Jen. Come on, hon.

JENNIFER. Okay, okay… So. Like…guess what, Mom? Big news! Remember those petitions you helped me write? Well, finally *finally* the school's letting us have a dance. For Valentine's Day. Like we've only been begging for 2 years! But now they –

DANIEL. Slow down, Jen. Give her time to absorb what you're saying.

JENNIFER. *(more slowly, using gestures)* – Valentine's Day. Hearts, flowers, romance – *totally* retro, but it's gonna be awesome! I am so pumped! Don't worry, there'll be chaperones, some teachers, a few mothers… What do you think?

DANIEL. 'Think…think…mo-ther.'

JENNIFER. Pardon?

DANIEL. '…Mo-ther. Me.'

JENNIFER. What does *that* mean???

DANIEL. Ask her. She's the only one who knows what she wants to say. Go on. You'll figure it out.

JENNIFER. All right, all right. God, this is worse than French! …'Mother.' You said, 'mother.'… I *know* you're my mother, Mom. Like, what about it?

DANIEL. '…Dance. Mo-ther.'

JENNIFER. You want to come to the dance?

(DANIEL nods, smiles.)

Like, be a chaperone, you mean?

(DANIEL nods again. JENNIFER goes into a panic.)

She can't do that. She can't! Everyone'll think she's a retard. She can't come to the dance. I'd die.

(**DANIEL** *gets tearful.*)

You're not going to cry...?! Daniel, why are you doing this? You're supposed to be helping me!

DANIEL. I *am* helping. I'm your mom now. You just told me you're ashamed of me, that you don't want me at your dance. I get the picture. Maybe I can't talk, but I can feel.

JENNIFER. This is really freaking me out. What am I going to do if she cries?

DANIEL. What does she do when *you* cry?

JENNIFER. (*considers, then moves close to* **DANIEL**, *awkwardly puts her arm around him*) I'm sorry, Mom. I didn't mean to make you feel bad. Sure, you can be a chaperone if you want. I mean, like, you're the one who taught me how to dance, you *should* be there. Anyway, Mom...you know...I love you.

THE TWELFTH DAY

(**ANNA** *and the* **APHASIC PATIENT** *are trying to play chess – but it's far from a conventional game.*)

ANNA. (*struggling for words to describe the accident*) Head headfrights – fights! Car sim- simmin arrow me! Daaaaar-byss. Ahhhhh...naaa cashimpa!

APHASIC PATIENT. (*fluently*) Oh, so that, why not, I know just how you want to everything and then, potatoes, okay, it's like that and rain jumps, poogel boogel day and night, sleeping English, and then go to possible, naturally, very nice.

(*They stare at each other with strained false smiles. Then he moves a chess piece. Triumphantly:*)

Heck and heck-mate!

THE FIFTEENTH DAY

JENNIFER. *(sitting beside her mother)* ...And that French test, Mom? The one I thought I was gonna fail? I got an 87. 87!

ANNA. Ohhhh! ...Ele-vator!!

(plants a kiss on the top of her daughter's head)

THE TWENTIETH DAY

(DANIEL is visiting ANNA and playing a recording of his concert.)

DANIEL. We had a full house. And my low notes? Rich as cream. I taped it for you.

(ANNA listens, then starts humming or singing along, perfectly in tune. Elated, he runs to get the therapist.)

Listen! She's singing! It's the aria I was rehearsing before the accident.

SPEECH THERAPIST. Oh yes, yes, lovely. You see, the musical area of the brain is located in the right hemisphere. It's the left part that's damaged.

DANIEL. She remembers, though...! And she's talking so much better than she did at first.

SPEECH THERAPIST. She's an incredibly hard worker.

DANIEL. So – are we talking weeks? Months? Because she has research to finish. And she gives lectures all over the country – the world.

SPEECH THERAPIST. I wish I had a crystal ball...!

DANIEL. You don't mean...she could stay like this...forever?

SPEECH THERAPIST. Oh no. She'll improve. But how much? In what ways? We really can't say. But what you're bringing to her – your music – is a great gift, a very special kind of communication. And she knows it. Do you hear? She's still singing with you.

DANIEL. ...Amazing! She really was listening all those times I rehearsed...!

(adds his voice to **ANNA***'s and the recording as he returns to her bedside)*

That's the way, darling. Sing, sing with me.

THE TWENTY-EIGHTH DAY

(Classroom: **BILL** *stands beside a locked box. Almost imperceptibly, the box seems to move, as if something were inside it.)*

BILL. Keep your eyes on this box. Watch carefully. Now. Now. Did you see it move? Is something inside? How can you know? You, my friends, are trapped in the famous paradox of Schrödinger's cat! Yes, I confess, a cat was placed in here twenty minutes ago. Aha! Now you think you might have heard a meow, or the sound of claws scratching against wood... But did you? Or is it just your imagination? Think hard now: we're talking life, we're talking death. Because inside this enigmatical box is a device that can release a noxious gas, killing the cat instantly. And what triggers the device? A random event, the spontaneous decay of an atom. Has the event occurred? Has the gas been released? Is the cat alive now, or dead? You can't say, can you? Because as long as we don't open the box, there's no way to be certain and the animal is neither alive *nor* dead, but exists in a third realm, on a different plane altogether, in a limbo of pure possibility that contains *both* extremes simultaneously: life and death, life and death, commingled.

(pause)

Now. Should we open it? Are you curious?

(starts to unlock the box, then stops)

But we still wouldn't be sure, would we? You know what curiosity does to a cat!

THE FORTIETH DAY

(**ANNA** *is sitting opposite the* **SPEECH THERAPIST** *in a therapy room. Throughout the session, she struggles for the right words.*)

(*Nearby: The* **APHASIC PATIENT** *also responds to the questions but his language is limited to the following:*)

"*Yes yes*"
"*Hellllp!!!*"
"*Thassit*"
"*Shit!*"
"*No way*"
"*Wow!!!*

(*He may be encouraging* **ANNA** *or giving his own answers to the questions or reacting to hers: any option can work but his responses should be chosen to provide a musical [and, where possible, humorous] counterpoint.*)

SPEECH THERAPIST. Again, what is your name?

ANNA. Aaaaa –

SPEECH THERAPIST. Yes, yes. Aaaaaaa –

ANNA. Aaa – starmer.

SPEECH THERAPIST. You're an astronomer, yes, but that's not your name. Your name also begins with A. A for Aaaa – Aaaa —

ANNA. Aaaa – Aaaa – na!

SPEECH THERAPIST. Anna! Good! That's your name. Okay, let's move on. I'm going to ask you some questions and you'll answer with yes or no. All right?

ANNA. Right.

SPEECH THERAPIST. Here we go. Listen carefully. Do children cry?

ANNA. ...No. ...Yes!

SPEECH THERAPIST. Children cry, right. Do cats like milk?

ANNA. ...Milk...yesmilk.

SPEECH THERAPIST. Excellent. Do dogs bark?

ANNA. Yes. No. Yes, bark yes!

SPEECH THERAPIST. Very good. Are you a dog?

ANNA. …Dog? Noooooo. No way.

SPEECH THERAPIST. Right again! Are you a man?

(**ANNA** *pauses; thinks.*)

Are you a man?

ANNA. No-man!

SPEECH THERAPIST. So. Are you a woman?

(**ANNA** *looks confused.*)

Are you a woman, Anna?

ANNA. ….An-naa wom. Woman.

SPEECH THERAPIST. Yes! You are a woman. And do you have children?

ANNA. Wom…wom-baby.

SPEECH THERAPIST. Your daughter?

ANNA. Yes!

SPEECH THERAPIST. What is her name?

(**ANNA** *searches for it.*)

Your daughter's name is –

(**ANNA**, *pained, can't find it.*)

Her name is Jenn – , Jenn –

ANNA. Jenn…Jenn-fer!

SPEECH THERAPIST. Your daughter, Jennifer. Wonderful. Let's try a few more. …Where do you live?

(**ANNA** *can't find it.*)

Do you live in New York?

ANNA. That's it!

SPEECH THERAPIST. So. Tell me: Where do you live?

ANNA. New…newapple!

SPEECH THERAPIST. You mean the Big Apple?

ANNA. Yes! BigNewYor-ple!

SPEECH THERAPIST. The Big Apple, New York. Great! And what is high up, over New York, in the sky?

ANNA. *(eagerly)* Sky moon.

SPEECH THERAPIST. The moon is in the sky, yes. And what else?

ANNA. Twinks…twinkles.

SPEECH THERAPIST. The stars?

ANNA. Stars stars orabora!!

SPEECH THERAPIST. Ora bora?

> *(**ANNA** nods; the **THERAPIST** ponders.)*

…Ora bora…

ANNA. Ora bor-is!

SPEECH THERAPIST. …Au-ro-ra bor-e-alis?

> *(**ANNA** nods enthusiastically.)*

Did I say that right?

ANNA. Verygood.

SPEECH THERAPIST. Beautiful work, Anna.

> *(prepares to leave)*

I'll see you tomorrow.

ANNA. Nogo. Wait. Want – want –

SPEECH THERAPIST. What is it? What do you want?

ANNA. Want – Want – oboe! No. El-bow! Nooo! Want want–

> *(**DANIEL** and **JENNIFER** appear, unnoticed, in the doorway.)*

SPEECH THERAPIST. Take it slowly.

ANNA. Lo. Yellow – no! Telfo.

SPEECH THERAPIST. The telephone?

ANNA. *(increasingly agitated)* No! Tell-toe. Toto. Toco–

> *(She continues circling around the word she wants – tecco, tesso, etc. – as the **SPEECH THERAPIST** quietly talks to **JENNIFER** and **DANIEL**.)*

SPEECH THERAPIST. She knows what she wants to say but she's lost the words. They're scattered over the terrain of her mind and without cues she can't retrieve the ones she needs. Imagine a violent wind tearing all the clothing from your closet and sending it flying to the four corners of the earth. You need your blue socks. That's all. Two matching blue socks. But where would you look for them? Everything's whirling around, tangled up, in chaos. She struggles; she finds one word here, another there, but then she can't string them together to express herself. What's happened to her is earth shattering. It's more than a problem with language. Her entire inner world has come apart.

ANNA. *(still driving toward her goal)* Tellco! Telso! Sco, sco!

JENNIFER. *(bursting into the room)* She wants her telescope!

ANNA. Jenn-fer!

Blackout

Scene Three

(Lights up on **BILL** *addressing his class, using an empty glass and one filled with milk as props, a slide of the Milky Way behind him.)*

BILL. Is she going to be "all there"? I don't know. But during a solar eclipse, the sun is still there, isn't it? And when a star collapses in on itself, isn't that star still there? We have to make the connections. It's all hooked up: the macrocosm and the microcosm, the inter-stellar dust and the dust that our bodies will become, the dark matter of the universe and the dark matter of the brain, the black hole in the cosmos and the black hole into which we will be thrown at the end. And leading our minds backward and forward from earth to heaven and from heaven to earth, we have been given a trail, a river, a bridge, the *via lactea* – billions of stars in a luminous galaxy.

(pours milk back and forth from glass to glass)

Galaxy, from "*galactos*," and "*lactos*" from "*galactos*," meaning –

(pours it into his mouth)

– milk.

(As lights go down there, two candles are lit in **ANNA**'s *home.)*

*(***DANIEL*** has almost finished setting the table and is placing a bottle of champagne in an ice bucket.* **ANNA** *watches admiringly. Throughout, she still searches for words but usually manages to communicate. And although she walks without impediment, she is not well-coordinated. Both try to keep the atmosphere "normal.")*

ANNA. You…ever-thing?

DANIEL. I alone.

ANNA. Cook too?

DANIEL. You could say that.

ANNA. No cook...pre – pre – pre-fore!

DANIEL. Pizza!...pre-fore

ANNA. Now...exper.

DANIEL. Me? An expert? Wait till you taste it!

ANNA. You cook. Exper – man.

DANIEL. Expert man...?

ANNA. Exper – sci! Sci!

DANIEL. Sigh. You're relieved I can cook?

(She shakes her head.)

Sigh... psy-cho? I'm psycho to try and cook?

ANNA. *(laughs)* Sci experman... Sci-an-exper—

DANIEL. Oh! A scientific experiment!

ANNA. Confabulations!

DANIEL. Confabulations to you, too! We'll get through this, hon. We'll be fine. Nothing's changed.

ANNA. Oh ho! *Big* change! Like earthcake! Allfall down. Very dis-disaster. Break! you me.

DANIEL. You think we're going to break up?

ANNA. No bed- bedding ring. Easy talkout – walk out.

DANIEL. Why? We never needed a law to keep us together.

ANNA. New law. Law – pits – pity.

DANIEL. No. Love.

ANNA. True?

DANIEL. True...glue.

(ANNA grabs for him, starts kissing wildly, wanting to express herself physically, without the burden of words. But she's forgotten exactly what to do. She's all over him, like a child, polymorphous perverse. He responds at first, then becomes unnerved by her anarchic passion. Gently he extricates himself.)

Wait, darling. Wait. Wait.

ANNA. Wait why?

DANIEL. Champagne – to celebrate your first night home.

ANNA. Cel-rate yes! Night. Home. Betternow fex!

DANIEL. *(distracted as he begins opening the bottle)* …better – ?

> *(He pops the cork; the champagne fizzes up.)*

ANNA. Fizzzzzz bubble!

> *(He pours. She holds up her glass to catch the champagne.)*

See? Anna glass for catch fizzlove.

DANIEL. *(filling his own glass)* You always did love champagne.

ANNA. Listen me! Daniel pour. Rain pour. You-me – fex! Fex!!

DANIEL. Ohhhh. Fex!

ANNA. *(nods; a big smile)* Now!

DANIEL. I may have forgotten how.

ANNA. I perfect memory that!

> *(They clink glasses; she is too forceful, and the glass breaks.)*

Stoop – stoop stupid! Cumsy!

DANIEL. *(wiping the spill)* Don't worry. It's nothing.

ANNA. Me. Me nothing.

DANIEL. Don't be ridiculous.

ANNA. Meglass. Break. Bitty pieces. Nofix. Neverfix.

DANIEL. Forget it, will you, Anna?

ANNA. Forget yes. Forget everystar. Forget words, shames–names! And shine in sty – spy – *sky*! Skyyyy!

DANIEL. The doctor said it takes time.

ANNA. Take shovel! Fill holesin head. Stu – pid. Dummy. Brain brain brain – e-clipse!!

DANIEL. Don't, Anna! You're killing yourself.

ANNA. Good. Die.

DANIEL. Well, that *is* stupid! A glass breaks and you want to die! Where's your willpower?

ANNA. You power! You talk meaning clear. Me gob – gobble-gook. Head…dead!

DANIEL. No. No! Your head is not dead! It's just the words – they're floating around inside. You'll find them again, you will! You will!

ANNA. *(breaking down)* When?? WHEN?

DANIEL. Please, please don't give up. I'd never forgive myself. I screamed you out of the house, right into that car. It's all my fault.

ANNA. You? No no, me! *Me* fault. Full anger, run darbyss. Stars…stars crash down.

DANIEL. Tell me what you want. I'll do anything I can.

ANNA. Want – want working.

DANIEL. You want to go back to teaching?

ANNA. No possible now teach class. Want – con. Go con..

DANIEL. You want to be at my next concert?

ANNA. Yes!! No. Con – con… Want con- fiss –

DANIEL. Confidence?

ANNA. Con-fiss pay. Pay ree. Tow – el. Pay towel.

DANIEL. Paper towel?

ANNA. *(more and more agitated)* Eye towel payree. Payree! Star con-fiss fly paper–

DANIEL. Flypaper???

ANNA. *(long pause; tries again, very deliberate)* Fly. Confiss. Star. Payree. …Jenn-fer! High up up 8-7! 8-7!

DANIEL. Her French test?

ANNA. Yes!

DANIEL. *(working it out)* French test… French… Pay-ree – Paris! Eye towel–Eiffel Tower! Flypaper. …Fly to Paris – read your paper – at the conference!

ANNA. Give five!

(They slap hands.)

DANIEL. Well, why not? You have three months. You might be able to make it.

ANNA. Work! Will!

DANIEL. I'm with you, darling. We'll fly together.

ANNA. Fly you…flyme, high high! Fex! Fly now!

*(She blows out the candles and the stage goes black as they move into each other's arms. In the darkness, **BILL**'s voice is heard.)*

BILL. Lights out. Total darkness. Can you see me? No – but
I'm here, I exist, like a black hole, a mass of matter so
dense, so compressed, that no light can escape from it.
But inside the hole, where your eyes, where even the
most powerful telescope cannot penetrate, the light is
shining, the light is simply trapped inside, unable to
reveal itself…

Scene Four

(Spotlight on **ANNA**. *She remains in the center while other characters move in and out from the periphery. She keeps trying to respond but usually doesn't even have time to form a word before she's barraged by someone else.)*

(Underscoring the live assault is a running tape of recorded voices and sounds, including ringing phones, news, music, sports events, answering machines, political announcements, commercials, etc.)

(The scene should move quickly and build to a hallucinatory intensity. Lines may be repeated and voices overlapped to create the effect.)

WAITER. Our specials today are cream of *pomodoro* soup, the *penne* with *porcini* and *sugo di cavolfiori*, salmon that have smothering in the leeks, and wild hen glazed with honey.

ANNA. …Okay.

WAITER. Okay w*hat??*

(louder and slower as if she were deaf, sometimes illustrating)

Soup *di pomodoro*, tomato, maybe you say tomahto. *Penne – pasta. Con porcini*, the mushrooms, and *sugo di cavolfiori* – sauce from flowers of the collie. Then we have the salmon – fish – river – high Omega-3. Or wild hen – like chicken!

(squawks to demonstrate)

DANIEL. Anna. I can't read this message. When is that callback?! Where? What time?

JENNIFER. Hey, Ma, teacher conferences! You gotta sign up.

BILL. Just wanted to let you know that Herbert and Holden are organizing a panel to discuss Neutrinos and they asked me to ask you if you want to –

WOMAN FRIEND. I will come to your house, all right? Then we will meet Nina at the museum. We will see the Cézanne show. Many paintings. Beautiful paintings. And after, we can have tea in the garden. Won't that be nice?

TICKET SELLER. Tickets available orchestra mezzanine balcony January 26, 27, 30 evening, or February 2 matinee and evening, partial view only. Which date, please? Which section? What price?

DANIEL. Anna, your group therapy starts in ten minutes.

GUEST AT PARTY. Well, hello, hello. No, don't say a word. I can see in your eyes that you hate this party, too. Why don't we sneak away and go dancing at the Rainbow Room?

ANNA. Rainbow yes. U-nick!

GUEST AT PARTY. *(insulted)* Eunuch?!

ANNA. U – nique! Rainbow u – nique!

BILL. Hey, Anna. *Science Times* today. All about the extrasolar –

ACQUAINTANCE. I know just what you're going through, really I do. I had strep throat and bronchitis last year – yes, a double dose! – and I couldn't get out a word, not a single word, it was hell, really – pure hell! And it lasted two full weeks! So I know just how it feels, and if you ever want to talk to someone about the agony of–

JENNIFER. Mom, I need a raise in my allowance, mine is so 1980s, I mean, movies don't cost a dollar anymore!

PERSON GIVING DIRECTIONS. You go out, walk 3 blocks north to the subway station and take the number 1 to 86th street, then walk uptown 4 blocks and turn right – I mean, left. Then you walk 2 more blocks, and you'll be at 301 W. 90th Street, right near Riverside Drive, right where you want to be. Now if you prefer the bus, you can take the 11 uptown and change for the cross-town –

(**ANNA** *screams, overwhelmed and in despair.*)

(*ELSEWHERE: Lights come up on the* **SPEECH THERA-PIST.**)

SPEECH THERAPIST *(addressing the audience)* She's like Sisyphus, rolling language up a hill. She has to search for every word and once she finds it, she struggles to hold it in her mind, then move it from her mind into her mouth, and from her mouth into sounds that can be understood. Can you imagine doing that every time you speak? Can you understand what a strain every conversation is? Someone asks me what kind of work I do. "I'm a speech therapist," I'd say. What could be easier? But if I had to pronounce every word backwards—

(scrupulously)

My. A. Ceeps tis-par-et.

(directly to audience)

You try it. Where were you born? City and state. Backwards. Go on. Let me hear you.

(waits for responses, ad libs if necessary: "Out loud." "I mean it. Try." "Don't be timid. Give it a shot." Etc.)

You see? The words don't come automatically anymore. Not even the simplest thing. Like your name. Try it. Backwards.

(The audience will start to respond but **ANNA** *gets there first.)*

ANNA Anna! Anna!

(The **SPEECH THERAPIST** *beams at her with pride.)*

Blackout

INTERMISSION

Scene Five

(Lights up on **ANNA** *at home, fussing with the room and herself in preparation for* **BILL** *'s first visit, setting out a teapot, cups, cake, etc., and humming "Some Enchanted Evening.")*

(Elsewhere: The **SPEECH THERAPIST** *sits with the* **APHA-SIC PATIENT***, helping him to read.)*

APHASIC PATIENT. *(slowly, with eccentric rhythm and accent)* "One day, when HennyPennywas scra-scra-scrap – "

SPEECH THERAPIST. – scratching.

APHASIC PATIENT. – "scratch-ing among the leavesinthe-barnyard, an ache – ache! – a-corn dropped fromatree and hit! hit! her on the head."

SPEECH THERAPIST. "Oh goodness gracious me!"…Go on.

APHASIC PATIENT. "Ohgoodnessgracious me!"

SPEECH THERAPIST. Good.

(The doorbell rings. **ANNA** *freezes, then composes herself, opens the door.)*

ANNA. Bill hell-hello! So happy seeyou.

BILL. *(horribly uncomfortable)* Oh yes, me, too, hello, hi. Wow. You – you look terrific. Really. You look just like yourself! I mean, not that you're *not* yourself but what happened was so awful, *unspeakable* – I mean –

ANNA. *(ushering him in)* Come sit. …Teacup cake?

BILL. Teacup – ?

(stares; gets it)

Sure, I'll have some tea. No cake. I'm watching my middle now, intensely watching, especially since I started this new study at the observatory. You know about it, don't you?

ANNA. Know nothing…zero!! from – <u>about</u> you.

BILL. *(oblivious; settling in)* Well, I'll tell you then.

ANNA. Tell – Tell –

(blurting)

Why no visit??!!

BILL. *(stumbling over himself)* Why…no…visit?…Oh. Well. You know how it is, work work work, double duty in the classroom, student conferences, faculty meetings, trying to write a paper, no sleep, time disappearing and –

ANNA. Shit!

BILL. What?

ANNA. Shitbull – Bill.

BILL. I guess…that's…my name.

(She pours tea, while elsewhere:)

APHASIC PATIENT. "Hennypennycr – cry out: 'The sky is failing.'"

SPEECH THERAPIST. Falling.

APHASIC PATIENT. Falling.

(In **ANNA***'s place:)*

ANNA. Working.

BILL. Like a dog. That's what I was saying –

ANNA. I. I working. My paper. From before axfall – <u>acci-dent</u>. Read paperyou, okay? Daniel no understand theory. You Bill fatpig.

BILL. Fat – ?

ANNA. <u>Guinea</u> pig, guinea pig!

(gets her manuscript, while elsewhere:)

APHASIC PATIENT. "'I must go and tell the King.' So she buriedalong and buriedalong and buriedalong – "

SPEECH THERAPIST. Hurried. Hurried along. That's what you're doing. Take your time.

(In **ANNA***'s place:)*

ANNA. Here. Hot press. First time readloud.

(reading haltingly, with odd inflections and errors)

ANNA. *(cont.)* My paper tired – <u>title</u>. "Cos-mic HideAnd-Seek, Pen – <u>Pin</u>-the-Tail-OnTheDar- Dark ness, and Blind Man's Butt – no! no! <u>Buff</u>!"

BILL. *(embarrassed; ignoring the error)* Terrific metaphor! The search for missing matter as a game. Go on.

ANNA. *(as before)* "Children's games, child's pray – <u>play</u>. But that is exactly our sit-u-a-tion vis-a-visa the cos-mos. Con-fun-fronted by the miseries – <u>mysteries</u> of in-fin-ity space, the blackness in which mostofthe universe is high – hiking – <u>hiding</u>, we speak – no! – we <u>seek</u>! <u>*seek*</u>!"

(flings down paper)

Awful. Too hard!

BILL. I didn't realize. God, Anna!

ANNA. *(bitterly)* No God. Stars! Bad stars!

BILL. I could read the paper for you…

ANNA. No! I working years, years! Now fine – <u>fin-ally</u> come prizehonor, I go confiss for U-nite State, show science stars to world!

BILL. But you can't stand in front of two thousand people and read like that.

ANNA. You want light. *My* light.

BILL. No, no, I don't. I want you to shine in your own.

ANNA. *(erupting)* Own! Alone! I missing! You hi-hi-hiding! Why no seekme? Why?!?

BILL. I'm sorry, Anna! I'm sorry!

ANNA. Terror – <u>terrible</u> no talking, nightmirror! And I…I sicktrouble, wanting work, conversion – <u>con-ver-sa-tion</u> from friend astarmy.

BILL. You're right, it's true: I wasn't there for you.

ANNA. Lost in stars!

BILL. I could kick myself now; I do kick myself. I just kept putting it off. I was scared I wouldn't know what to say, what to do. But I thought of you every day. And I missed you; we all missed you. The students are sick to death of me. Everybody wants you back. Gabriel's not hiring anyone till you make your plans and…what's his name?…wants to use your research in his article on dwarf stars.

ANNA. Who?

BILL. Oh, what's his name…in our department…short… glasses…it's on the tip of my tongue. You know. Had a hair transplant…

ANNA. Nathan.

BILL. Right! Nathan.

(They regard each other wryly, **ANNA** *very proud of herself, while elsewhere:)*

APHASIC PATIENT. "So she hurriedalong and soon she met Co-ck-y Lo-ck-y." Cocky Locky?

SPEECH THERAPIST. Cocky Locky, that's what it says.

APHASIC PATIENT. *(a howl of pain)* "Warand Peace!" "King Leeeeear!" No Cocky Locky! Noooo! Noooo!

(The **APHASIC PATIENT** *flings book to floor and runs off, the* **THERAPIST** *following him.)*

ANNA. Now tell jerk – <u>work</u> you Bill. Observ-ty. Why?

BILL. I've been studying the cycle. Watching the stars go through it, birth to death. And guess what? They don't age any more gracefully than we do! So – I'm starting a new project – on middle-aged stars.

ANNA. *You* middleage crybaby – <u>crisis</u>.

BILL. That's it! My title: "Mid-star Crisis!" You're still fabulous.

ANNA. And you – still Billshit.

BILL. I love you, too. May I stay a while?

(She nods; he settles in.)

It turns out that middle-aged stars have exactly the same problems as middle-aged people. They experience more inner turbulence – indigestion, gas, ulcers. Their energy slackens, they move more slowly, lose their youthful glow, get washed out, dull. Even their waist lines thicken. I'm the living analogy. Look.

(He starts to pull his sweater off, but his head gets stuck in an armhole just as **JENNIFER** *jives in, humming, oblivious, her iPod playing music through headphones. Trying to extricate himself,* **BILL** *'s hand lands on a breast.)*

JENNIFER. *(yelling and pushing him away)* Hey! Hands off, dude! Don't play perv with me!

BILL. *(getting his head through the neckhole)* Sorry, Jen. I couldn't see, I didn't mean to –

JENNIFER. Oh sure, sure – it was an 'accident.' Yeah – accident on purpose!

Scene Six

(That evening: lights up on DANIEL *rehearsing his audition song, stopping and starting to perfect it. The aria continues under scene and then fades out.)*

(At the same time: lights rise on JENNIFER *and* ANNA.*)*

JENNIFER. Like, I'm standing on the subway and all of a sudden I feel a hand creeping over my butt. Or a bunch of boys are goofing around behind me in school and next thing I know my bra is being snapped. It's totally vomitacious. I mean, guys are just so…primitive. All they want to do is try out their new hormones on you! I get really weirded out but…I don't want everyone to think I'm a dork.

*(*ANNA *nods.)*

I'm even scared to go to the dance. Like, what if some boy presses his – presses into me, starts grinding, you know, or puts his hands where he shouldn't?

*(*ANNA *picks up* JENNIFER*'s hand, slaps it; nods emphatically.)*

Slap his hand? You don't do that in modern times, Mom!

ANNA. "Body my body."

JENNIFER. I'm talking about *my* body, mom.

ANNA. Me, too.

JENNIFER. Well, I don't want to talk about your body. Or your brain. I mean, aphasia's not the only problem in the world.

ANNA. Grow up. Hard.

JENNIFER. Like, did you have to deal with all this stuff, boys hitting on you and –

ANNA. No hit. Never hit!

JENNIFER. Chill, Mom! I mean 'hit' like guys trying to hook up, you know, put the moves on you. God, I don't know what's worse, if they want to make out or they don't. Like, what if nobody asks me to dance? What if all my friends get asked and I have to stand there all night like a reject?

ANNA. No worry flower on wall.

JENNIFER. Maybe I just shouldn't go. I don't have anything to wear anyway. No offense, Mom, but my clothes look like they died last year! If I go to that dance, I need a killer dress.

ANNA. Cool dress.

JENNIFER. Hot, mom. I gotta look hot!

ANNA. Hot!? Boys touch hot.

JENNIFER. Oh god, Mom, you don't understand anything!

ANNA. *(starting to brush* **JENNIFER***'s hair)* Understand yes. Mix up. Teen-age. ...Hair straw!!

JENNIFER. Right, beat me up a little more, I need it.

(as her hair is pulled)

Owww! You're killing me!

ANNA. No kill. Trans-form. Get make-out – No, no, <u>make-up</u>! Put on cosmics. I mean – <u>cos-metics</u>.

JENNIFER. Isn't your speech ever going to get better, Mom?

ANNA. Maybe no. Forget words now. Big night come. Dancing fuck!

JENNIFER. Mother!!

ANNA. <u>Fun</u>! Dancing <u>fun</u>! Cool Jennfer.

JENNIFER. Hot, Mom! I want to look hot!

(Lights shift to **BILL***. He could be in the Observatory, standing against the night sky, brightly colored stars surrounding him. Or he might be in a lecture hall, making a PowerPoint demonstration, or using slides to illustrate his talk.)*

BILL. ...And just like human beings, stars travel through the life cycle: their evolution is even color-coded. Look! These blue stars are the young ones, hot, throbbing with passion; the yellows are less intense, a bit sedate already, with a hint of flab around the middle; the reds have become elderly, sending out their weary rays of light; and these white dwarf stars are burned out, cooling into brown and then black dwarfs, like dying embers. We used to believe that these stars were all that existed, and that our earth was at the center of everything. Now we know that we're just one infinitesimal planet drifting through an eternity of a hundred billion galaxies and a billion trillion stars...

Scene Seven

(Lights up on ANNA *with a* SALESWOMAN.*)*

SALESWOMAN. So. You're looking for a dress for your daughter. What size is she?

ANNA. ...Small – teen...

SALESWOMAN. Yes. But I need to know her size. ...A six? Four?

ANNA. *(guessing)* Six.

SALESWOMAN. Fine. A six. Now, what kind of dress are you looking for?

ANNA. Dance. Hot.

SALESWOMAN. A...hot...dance? Oh. You mean...for the summer? A light material, perhaps a chiffon?

ANNA. Pretty.

SALESWOMAN. All our dresses are pretty.

ANNA. Hot pretty! Cool! Hot!

SALESWOMAN. *(obviously thinks that* ANNA *is deranged, but tries to be polite)* Really, don't you think it would be better if you brought your daughter in with you?

ANNA. No! Heartdance. Surprise dress.

SALESWOMAN. I'm sorry, dear. Try Bloomingdale's.

(starts walking away; ANNA *grabs her arm)*

Don't you dare touch me! I'll call the police!

ANNA. Patient, please, patient.

SALESWOMAN. Ohhhh. You're a patient! I thought so. Drugs. And with a child, too. Shame on you. No wonder you can't talk straight!

ANNA. Nodrugs, no. Choc-late. Flowers. Holl-day. Holl-dance. Holl–

SALESWOMAN. Holland????...You're Dutch?!

ANNA. *(seizing the opportunity)* Dutchyes!

SALESWOMAN. Well, why didn't you say so?

(speaking slowly)

Come with me. I'll show you everything we have… Oh, I adore tulips!

(Lights come up on the **APHASIC PATIENT***, reading words that convey emotions, trying to express them in both his voice and face.)*

APHASIC PATIENT. *(overlapping the* **SALESWOMAN** *'s last line)*
I a door – a door??? – ADORE. I ADORE you.
I hot hit – HATE you.
I scar – scarred – SCARED.
I SORROW.
I pass-passing-PASSION. I PASSION!
I pappy – peppy – heppy – HAPPY. HAPPY!
I glow – GLORY.

(with powerful feeling)
I GLORY!

Scene Eight

(A **REPORTER** *interviews* **ANNA** *at home while* **DANIEL** *hovers.)*

REPORTER. I gather you're making a marvelous recovery.

ANNA. Very struggle.

REPORTER. How long has it been since the accident?

ANNA. Three – five days – years.

DANIEL. Months. Five months.

REPORTER. You still have therapy?

ANNA. Yes yes. Many therapy. Everyday. But now also auto-mo-bile.

DANIEL. I think she means 'autonomous'.

ANNA. Auto-mobile! I auto. Self. And mo-bile. Moving. Self-move.

REPORTER. Oh. Great! I get it!

DANIEL. Yes, we can finally see the light at the end of the tongue – tunnel! I mean, tunnel!

ANNA. Daniel – slip of tunnel. Aphasia catching!

REPORTER. Nooo! It's not contagious…is it???

ANNA. Everyone aphasia sometime. Too bad no vaccine for that, right?

REPORTER. But…but it's not like… measles or – ?

ANNA. No, no sweat. You perfect safe.

REPORTER. Well, I thought so, but– Anyway. Moving right along. You're still planning to deliver your paper in Paris?

ANNA. Oh yes! Im – imp – impotent.

DANIEL. Important. It's important to her.

ANNA. *Paper* important.

DANIEL. Right. Sorry, Anna.

ANNA. No problem.

REPORTER. How do you keep up with the newest discoveries?

ANNA. Con – fuser. No, no.

   (laughs)

   Con-pu-ter.

REPORTER. Yes, of course. Can you give me a general idea about the subject of your paper? Nothing too complicated. This is a human interest story, not a scientific article.

ANNA. Matter about cold and dark –

DANIEL. She's studying the dark matter question.

ANNA. Daniel! I explain. Darkmatter cosmos, yes. Universe hiding. Wheelchair man…great science, name… name… Daniel?

DANIEL. Stephen Hawking.

ANNA. Hawkman, right. He say two mystery only. One cosmos, one brain.

REPORTER. *(making notes)* Stephen Hawking. Mysteries of cosmos and brain. Do I have that right?

ANNA. *(encouraged to go on)* Yes! Manymissing between and between. No supper – No <u>sep-ar-ate</u> human and stardust. Same matter. Life part from alluniverse, connect ocean, water of body –

REPORTER. What is she trying to say?

DANIEL. She's saying that all human life is created from the same matter as –

ANNA. *(upset; to **DANIEL**)* Stop! No speak my thinking.

REPORTER. I'm sorry, I just didn't understand–

DANIEL. Anna, I was only trying to clarify what –

ANNA. I know, I know!

   *(holding back tears; to **REPORTER**)*

   Daniel veryhelp but he opera. I astarmer, I talk science.

DANIEL. You want me to go?

ANNA. Yes. No. Yes! Go make aria. I finish reporter.

DANIEL. Fine. I have a thousand things to do.

REPORTER. *(getting up)* That's all right. I need to leave anyway, it's getting late and –

ANNA. No. Please. Newspaper stay.

REPORTER. Really. I can come back on a better day.

DANIEL. *(deliberately; coldly)* There are no better days.

ANNA. …What?

REPORTER. I'm so sorry if I – Thanks very much. I'll phone…

(exits)

ANNA. *(still stunned)* …Daniel?

DANIEL. Who do you think you are, waving your hand like a goddam queen, ordering me to talk, not to talk, leave the room, "Go make aria!" Yes, your Majesty. At your service. Anytime, anywhere. You asked me to stick around for this interview, remember?

ANNA. No ask you put words in mouth.

DANIEL. How am I supposed to know when you want me to jump in? I can't read your mind. I just try to save your ass when I can!

ANNA. Now she write newspaper Anna no make sense.

DANIEL. Sometimes you *don't* make sense!

ANNA. Not true!

DANIEL. Yes, true. Face it. Sometimes only I can understand what you're saying. Or Jenny. We're used to you; we can figure out what you mean. But to other people? Half the time it sounds like…gibberish!

ANNA. I little words but you, you little heart. Hurting feel good. Anna weak, now you bigpants, walk cockcockcock.

DANIEL. Oh yeah, it's terrific for me. What power I have! I get to put you in a taxi, tell the driver where to go; I get to work with Jenny on her homework, talk to her teachers; I get to write the checks, talk to the doctors, write down your appointments: Oh, am I lucky! Mozart can wait! It's an honor to be your eyes, your ears, your crutch, your caretaker, your longtime companion –

ANNA. Stop!!!!! Years, years I *everything!* From auditions I call, I with love, I do in-fin-ity!

DANIEL. All right! I wouldn't have a career if you hadn't pushed me, insisted I audition, shamed me into rehearsing. Okay! So now we're even, right?... But what about the next ten years? The next twenty, thirty, FORTY YEARS?!!!

ANNA. Free man.

DANIEL. Free? Oh no, honey, I'm trapped in here with you. We're a team. The prisoner and the guard. The puppet and the puppeteer. Can't have one without the other. Think about it. What would you do if I walked out?

ANNA. ...Make new life.

DANIEL. You'd be fine without me?

ANNA. Super fine.

DANIEL. Really? All alone? "Auto-mobile?"

ANNA. Go! Go! Take freedom!

DANIEL. You don't have to ask me twice. I'm out of here!

(He wheels away and exits the room, gets a suitcase, starts packing. JENNIFER sees what he's doing, tries to stop him.)

JENNIFER. You're not gonna split, Daniel...?

DANIEL. It's too much for me. *She's* too much for me.

JENNIFER. No, no, don't say that! She's just getting back on her feet. I mean she was up there with the stars and then she had this tragic fall – like Oedipus, you know, except the gods didn't put out her eyes, they took away her language, and it wasn't the gods, it was luck, horrible luck, and just *imagine* how she feels!

DANIEL. That's all I've been doing for months.

JENNIFER. Please, please, don't bail on her. I'll help you more, honest, I'll learn how to cook, and I'll clean –

DANIEL. Don't worry. She'll be fine without me. Superfine, she said.

JENNIFER. Well, what do you expect her to say? We women have our pride! She needs you, she really does.

DANIEL. She needs someone – but she couldn't care less if it's me or the man in the moon.

JENNIFER. *You're* the man in the moon to her!....And to me.

DANIEL. Oh, Jen, don't you get upset now.

JENNIFER. But you'll be walking out on me, too.

DANIEL. This has nothing to do with you.

JENNIFER. Nothing? It's the story of my life! Men bailing on me.

DANIEL. Men? What men?

JENNIFER. Like – my real dad, duh?

DANIEL. Your father did not 'bail' on you. He had cancer. And you were two years old.

JENNIFER. He's still gone, isn't he? He couldn't help what happened, but you can. You walk out and I'll be stuck with everything. I'll have to be the daughter and the boyfriend and the secretary and the nurse and you know how I'll end up, don't you? I'll be one of those little old ladies who spend their whole lives taking care of their little old moms, and I'll never have a life of my own!

DANIEL. Don't, Jen, don't.

JENNIFER. I bet this happens all the time. Half a couple gets some horrible sickness and the other half can't handle it. But you? I really thought you really loved her.

DANIEL. Love's not everything.

JENNIFER. It isn't? So how come all the movies are about it? And the novels? And your operas! I know, I've seen them: they're all tragedies about love. The guys sweet-talk the women until they do a Molly Bloom yes yes yes, and you hear swirls of passion in the music, which is pretty cool, even if it *is* opera, and then the creeps run out on them. And the women go crazy. Or commit suicide. Or cough themselves to death.

DANIEL. Trust me, Jen. Your mother isn't going to die because I leave.

JENNIFER. She could. You're the great love of her life.

DANIEL. Oh yeah. Right.

JENNIFER. Right. "When he walked into the party and flashed that adorable smile at me, I turned into a romantic cliché – my knees went weak and my heart jumped over the moon."

DANIEL. She never said that.

JENNIFER. Yes, she did. She adores your smile. And your laugh. To this very day. And you make her really happy when you sing her to sleep at night. Her favorite is "*Some Enchanted Evening.*"

DANIEL. She told you all that?

JENNIFER. Only about twenty times.

DANIEL. In words?

> (**ANNA**, *who has overheard much of this, steps into the room.*)

ANNA. More. More than words.

JENNIFER. *(after a silence)* Omigod. Holy Moly! I have that damn final tomorrow. Pardon my French. But it *is* French. The final, I mean. See you guys later. *Bon soir.* Or *bon nuit.* Whatever.

> *(exits)*

DANIEL. You have something to say to me?

> (**ANNA** *nods, touches his arm. He moves away.*)

Well?

ANNA. *(in a murmur)* No want.

DANIEL. No want what?

> *(She reaches for him again; he brushes her off.)*

You sure could talk to that reporter. What's the matter now?

ANNA. Fraid.

DANIEL. Afraid? Of what?

ANNA. …No want you go, leaveAnna all own. Alone.

DANIEL. Jen's here.

ANNA. No. You. You! Want you!

DANIEL. Why?

ANNA. Very – very need you.

DANIEL. It's nice to be needed but…sorry…it's not enough.

ANNA. Very…love.

DANIEL. You don't show it. And I don't feel it. Not anymore.

ANNA. I know.

DANIEL. You know?! Then why? Why?

ANNA. …I…hiding.

DANIEL. From me?

ANNA. You. Yes.

> I am shame and des-pair.
>
> Rain of tears everyday.
>
> Feel beggar down ground,
>
> Only take take take!
>
> Emptyhand, nothing give.

DANIEL. Not true. You have something to give but – you don't. Not to me, anyway.

ANNA. Words words dis – disappear.

> Heart in jail.
>
> No can move love to mouth.

DANIEL. Try. I need you to try.

ANNA. You…Daniel…

> Wish on stars belove man Daniel.
>
> Wake up nightmirror,
>
> See face smiling bright, breathing life,
>
> Musicsong all morningnight.
>
> Big luck from me!

DANIEL. *(moved)* Big luck *for* you.

ANNA. Yes. Giant luck!

> *(flings her arms around him)*
>
> Thank you, thank you!

Scene Nine

(Lights up on the **APHASIC PATIENT**, *reading from a book or a computer screen, struggling through the lesson on prepositions.)*

APHASIC PATIENT. *(acting out words)*
AROUND. I walkaround the chair – AROUND...
DOWN. I look down atthefloor – DOWN DOWN DOWN
TO. I wave to the people – wave TO...wave TO the people...

(Lights fade there and rise on **JENNIFER**, *sitting at a vanity table, putting on make-up and listening to her ubiquitous iPod.)*

*(***DANIEL** *is offstage, rehearsing phrases from the Papageno/Papagena duet in* The Magic Flute.*)*

*(***ANNA** *enters and sits down next to* **JENNIFER**, *starts applying make-up, too. Both are in robes or slips or other undergarments.)*

ANNA. What music in head ears?

JENNIFER. What?

ANNA. *(shouting to be heard)* Music in head ears?!

JENNIFER. *(louder)* Rap!

ANNA. *(louder still)* Crap??

JENNIFER. *(topping her)* Rap!!!!

DANIEL. *(offstage)* Will you tone it down in there, please?

ANNA. *(gestures* **JENNIFER** *to shush)* Quiet. Daniel need concert – <u>concentrate</u>.

JENNIFER. His geezer music!

ANNA. And your rapmusic? Why so superfabulous superior?

JENNIFER. You wouldn't get it.

ANNA. Why no?

JENNIFER. Words. It's all words.

ANNA. Give.

JENNIFER. Get a life, Mom.

ANNA. Trying. Give.

(**JENNIFER** *hands over the iPod, puts headphones on* **ANNA,** *who listens, responds to the beat.*)

(*Elsewhere:*)

APHASIC PATIENT. I put my hand undernea – under… knee??? under-neath my chin! UNDERNEATH. I jump into the wa-ter. INTO. I jump INTO –

(*holds nose and jumps*)

ANNA. (*gasps, gasps again*) Words yes! Words perfect understand! 'Motherfuckin, motherfuckin, fuckin motherfuckin…'

JENNIFER. I knew you'd freak.

ANNA. (*hands back iPod*) Terr-ble. Sexist! Why no 'father-fuckin'?

JENNIFER. You don't care?

ANNA. Good beat, bad words. Same me.

JENNIFER. There you go, getting down on yourself again! Give yourself a break, mom. How many people get a second chance in life? But you, you're like a new person. That is totally cosmic, don't you think?

ANNA. Effin' awesome!

JENNIFER. (*noticing her mother's messy make-up*) Oh, gross! And you were the one who taught *me* how to color inside the lines!

(*starts to fix the make-up but* **ANNA** *grabs her wrist*)

ANNA. What this???

JENNIFER. You don't recognize it? God, Mom. Of all people! It's Orion's belt! I mean, I know you said I couldn't tattoo it on my ankle, but…

ANNA. But?

JENNIFER. Well, my wrist isn't my ankle. …And I did make honor roll… And all my friends were doing it last week – and I know, I know, I should have asked but – it's cool, right?

ANNA. ...Hot, Jennfer, hot.

JENNIFER. Thanks, mom. You're the best.

(elsewhere:)

APHASIC PATIENT. OVER. Sometimes God has to hit us over the head. OVER...

(looks up, down, around for God; then exits)

DANIEL. *(Offstage, begins Papageno's song, after the three boys bring in Papagena and sing: "Nun, Papageno, sich dich un," leaving a silence for female echo.)*
PA. PA PA PA PA. etc.

JENNIFER. He's really got the role?

ANNA. Sign on line.

JENNIFER. He could be a star. You'll be studying the stars and he'll be one.

ANNA. And you starry eye!

JENNIFER. Sweet! We'll be a family of stars! Far out!

ANNA. Very far.

JENNIFER. You really like the way he sings, don't you?

ANNA. Love.

DANIEL. *PA PA PA*

(At the silence left for Papagena's part, ANNA inserts her voice.)

ANNA. *PA PA PA*

DANIEL. *PA PA PA PA*

ANNA. *PA PA PA PA*

DANIEL. *PA PA PA PA PA PA PA PA*, etc.

(The duet continues until DANIEL enters. Together they sing the final phrases, ending with)

DANIEL/ANNA. *PA PA PA PA PA PA-GENO!*
PA PA PA PA PA PA-GENA!

(Music from The Magic Flute *continues as lights dim there and come up on BILL.)*

BILL. Press your ear to the cosmos and you hear it: the music of the spheres. Centuries ago, Pythagoras, listening in the night to the movements of the seven planets, made out the seven tones of the musical scale and exulted to know that harmony exists between heaven and earth, and that the universe sings, yes, it pulsates with rhythm; out of nothingness, out of its own motions, it makes a divine music, if you listen for it, and the celestial bodies dance...

(He dances.)

*(***JENNIFER*** enters the gym in her 'hot' dress. ***ANNA***, as chaperone, stands on the sidelines and watches.)*

*(***A YOUNG MAN*** enters and taps ***JENNIFER*** on the shoulder.)*

YOUNG MAN. Hey! Killer dress.

*(***JENNIFER*** smiles shyly.)*

Blows me away.

(She smiles again, at a loss for words.)

Dance?

JENNIFER. Okay.

(They dance.)

Scene Ten

(Sound: A jet airplane in flight. Over it, the end of **JEN-NIFER**'s *language tape is being played.)*

TAPE. French is a romance language, capable of express-ing many subtle shades of meaning. For this reason, it has always been considered the language of love and of diplomacy. It is spoken all over the world, in the Caribbean, Africa, Canada and naturally in France. We hope this tape has prepared you for your travels. *Voila. Un de ces jours nous nous recontrerons a l'Arc de Triomphe au Place d'Étoile! Bon Voyage!*

(A spotlight picks up **ANNA**, *dressed elegantly and wear-ing her restrung beads, at the International Conference in Paris. She is reading from her paper, speaking slowly into a microphone.)*

(If desired, she can be accompanied by translators into French and sign language. But both of these should with-draw at the point that she puts down her manuscript.)

ANNA. "…missing matter is not a hole – <u>wholly</u> accurate term. Part-i-cles of light that wonder – <u>wander</u> inside a black hole are kid-napped and be-come hostage to grave – <u>grav-ity</u>. But past mis-cal-cu-lations of light abyss – <u>ab-sorp-tion</u> have caused signif – i – cant un-der-esti-mates of the darkmatter problem. This can be partly solid – <u>solved!</u> by cor-rec-ting this miss – misery – <u>mistake</u>…!

(pained, she stops)

Mistakes. Too much.

(hesitates – a difficult moment)

Ladies and genmen, forgive.

Big words, astarmy.

Elephants on tongue.

(pauses, make a decision)

ANNA. *(cont.)* No science paper.

(puts down paper, speaks spontaneously)

Look at cosmos and you see
great spaces between stars.
Now, for me, spaces between words,
black holes listening, black holes talking.
I searching many true- <u>truth</u> I feel
but can not ex-press.
Ideas in head but pure – <u>poor</u> words…

(a confession, an acceptance)

I am aphasia,
Anna aphasia.

(pauses, brightens)

You know story "Alice Wonderland",
fall down black hole,
not dying but ex-plore new world.
Now better my o-pen heart.
Surprise!! in living, everyday.
I work for find shine of light.
Night sky beautiful
and missing
and mystery.
Wonder –
Wonder full.
I. You.
All world.
Speech less.

End of Play

See what people are saying about
NIGHT SKY...

"The enthralling *Night Sky*, running off-Broadway in Manhattan, may be the accomplished Susan Yankowitz's best play yet. Her first-hand knowledge of aphasia and exemplary research into astronomy are breathtaking as she embraces an insight of Stephen Hawking's that the two abiding unsolved mysteries are the brain and the cosmos. She makes a poetic and dramatic case for the resemblance or correspondence between the black holes of the universe and the dark recesses of the human brain, and unponderously enlightens us in her serious and humorous, wise and profoundly moving play."
– John Simon, *Bloomberg News*

"Susan Yankowitz's *Night Sky* is a rare thing: a play with a mind. It is also about the mind as universe, where language is internal astronomy. It shows us that more than hearts can be broken. ...The subject is astronomy. The subject is language. The subject is courage – and how all these fit together in a subtly patterned script of a life suddenly eclipsed by disaster. Don't miss this one."
– Toby Zinman, *Variety*

"...Most of the time, the audience is giggling and reveling in Yankowitz's clever word play and double entendres. It's like hearing the subtext rise to the surface, and there's no denying truth in subtext. A wonderfully crafted script and some stellar performances make the show a moving and poetic experience. Like the sky, it is a play of seemingly infinite depth."
– Adelina Anthony, *L.A. Times*

"Bursting with wit, intelligence and energy, *Night Sky* is a sharp, multi-layered exploration of the cosmos and human beings' place in it, using all the resources of theatre to address the limits of our understanding of physical and metaphysical universes. It's an illuminating work, not least in its exploration of gender issues while bringing a human dimension to the other-worldly speculations of science."
– Peter Cudmore, *The Scotsman*

"A mind lost in a black hole, groping for words in the spaces between the stars, struggling to communicate with 'elephants on the tongue' - this is the rich imagery of *Night Sky*, a fascinating and moving play, interweaving human tragedy and emotion with the enduring mystery of the cosmos... This extremely well-constructed play is a study of people on the edge, but it is also a study of the triumph of the human spirit. They survive, and through their tragedy become deeper and richer human beings. Even in a black hole, the light shines."
– Jenny Downthwaite, *Sunday Star*

"Watching this American playwright weave a web which ultimately binds man and the cosmos is a breathtaking experience. The depth of Yankowitz' research enables her to spin wonderful metaphors, creating a masterpiece which entertainingly enlightens audiences. To sum it all up, *Night Sky* is a simply celestial theatre experience."
– *Pretoria News*

"...A haunting, fascinating play, ...a must-see for the adventurous theater buff. The final word is like a signal – an unanswerable query released into the heavens."
– Dan Hulbert, *Atlanta Journal/Constitution*

"The play has beautiful language and images; multiple references to stars, skies, understanding and communication foreshadow the disaster to come. Yankowitz paints a deeply felt, realistic portrait of the fears and disappointments inherent in the painfully slow process of regaining speech and language skills."
– Pat Launer, *San Diego Theatre Scene*

"The most daring aspect of *Night Sky* is its willingness to contemplate the absence of speech as a benefit rather than a disability, the source of a renewed sense of wonder in minutiae, of personal achievement in every complete sentence, and of revelation in every verbal slip. ...The last word, the summing-up of Anna's attempt to deliver her paper, conveys both her inability and her scientist's sense of wonder at the universe –'speechless.'"
– Michael Feingold, *Village Voice*

"'Can you think without words?' That's one of many questions ringing through Susan Yankowitz's *Night Sky*, a play that reveals, explores and meditates upon the condition known as aphasia. Playwright Yankowitz has scripted several of the more adventurous productions seen in San Diego over the years — a revival of The Open Theatre's landmark *Terminal* at UC San Diego in 1996 and a beautifully unified and harrowing *A Knife in the Heart* at Sledgehammer in 2002. Here, medical realism, domestic naturalism, fantastical monologues, lectures by Anna and her astronomer colleague, are connected by parallel images of the physical universe and Anna's mental world. (After Anna is hit by a car) her language undergoes the equivalent of the Big Bang, words exploded and strewn all over a mental cosmos. We watch her terror when she realizes that what comes out of her mouth is not the word she wishes to say, her struggles as she attempts to relearn language, and her ultimate triumph when she accepts (and can express) a condition that has released her into a new and wonder-filled reality."
- Anne Marie Welsh, *North County Times*

"A sprawling, intensely interesting play with emotional urgency...an exploration of the whole nature of language, thinking, communication and the universe."
– Aileen Jacobsen, *New York Newsday*